Communicate with SYMBOLS

Dear Reader

Every day, people use all kinds of symbols to communicate with each other. When symbols are designed and presented well, they enable us to convey messages quickly and efficiently. For example, think about how you would design a symbol for a new app icon that must instantly convey what it is to browsing users. In Chapter 5, you'll find some ideas that may help you to design effective symbols like icons and logos, as well as eye-catching advertisements.

GREEN BY HEART, CHARITABLE BY NATURE.

GREEN HEARTS RECYCLERS

In Chapter 2, see how traditional symbols are used artistically in Aboriginal art. On pages 8–9, meet Mary Brumby, a successful indigenous artist from South Australia. Mary has kindly allowed me to reproduce one of her magnificent works of art, *Karu*.

I hope that you enjoy viewing and reading about just some of the many uses for symbols in this book.

Sharon Parsons

My sincere thanks to the following people for their time, information, images and enthusiasm for this book:

Mary and Ronnie Brumby,
Echo Hill, Pukatja Homeland,
South Australia, Australia

Helen Johnson, Iwantja Arts and Crafts,
Indulkana, South Australia, Australia

Dianne and Phil Sidebottom,
Green Hearts Recyclers, Melbourne,
Australia

NELSON
CENGAGE Learning™
For learning solutions, visit **cengage.com.au**

Contents

Communicate with SYMBOLS

1 Why We Design Symbols

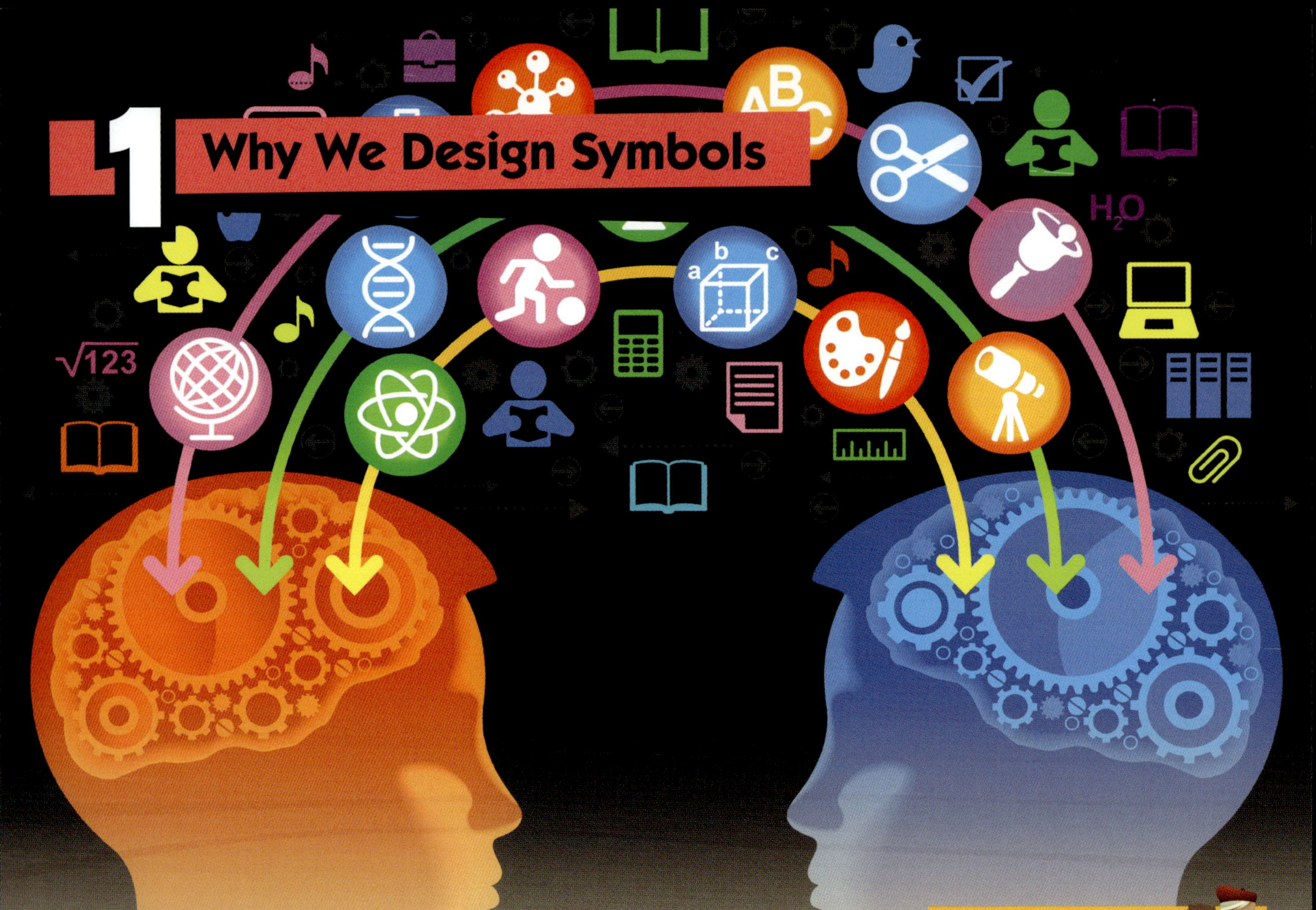

What Is a Symbol?

A symbol is something that represents something else. Symbols are a visual way of communicating information simply. A good symbol will communicate meaning without the need for language. A symbol might be a letter, a graphic or a physical object.

SYMBOLIST

A person who studies symbols or uses them to communicate ideas.

Designing Effective Symbols

Symbols are one of the most effective forms of communication because when they are designed well, they can easily communicate the same thing to many different people. Place a stylised image of a kangaroo on a clothing label, or a kiwi on the tail of an aircraft, and most people would know which country they represent. A well-designed symbol quickly conveys meaning to an audience, no matter what language they speak. That makes symbols a powerful means of communication in a world of many languages.

SEMIOTICS

The theory and study of signs and symbols used to communicate ideas in language.

Animal Symbols

Music Symbols

Currency Symbols

Symbols for Services

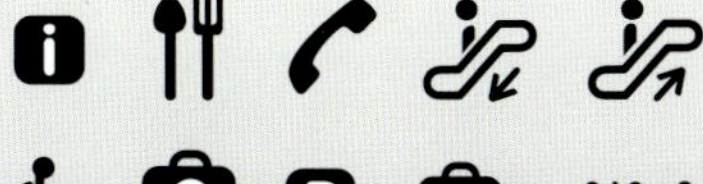

Ban Symbols

Safety Symbols

Road Symbols

Symbols for Charts

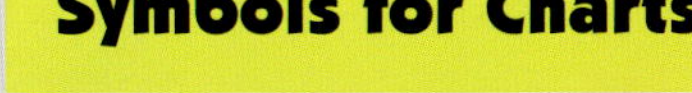

Technology Symbols

Environment Care Symbols

Weather Map Symbols

2 Symbols in Aboriginal Art

Traditional Australian Aboriginal and Torres Strait Islander art isn't only an artistic endeavour. It's also a visual means of using symbols to record traditional stories and information of importance to Indigenous Australian peoples. It is an artistic tradition using symbols to communicate information about where to find waterholes, animals, sacred sites, and to convey stories about the Dreaming. Artists depict the landscape and stories through combinations of colour, lines, dots, circles and other shapes.

In ancient times, this knowledge was passed from generation to generation by painting symbols on bodies and on the sand. Rock art was also used to communicate Dreaming stories and other local history and legends, using natural plant and mineral substances to paint figures and symbols on rock surfaces. But in recent times, the symbols that are important to the traditions of each Indigenous Australian group have been recorded in more contemporary forms, such as acrylic paint on canvas.

Wavy lines are used for flowing water, sand hills and a river or creek bed.

Concentric circles are used to show meeting places, campsites or waterholes.

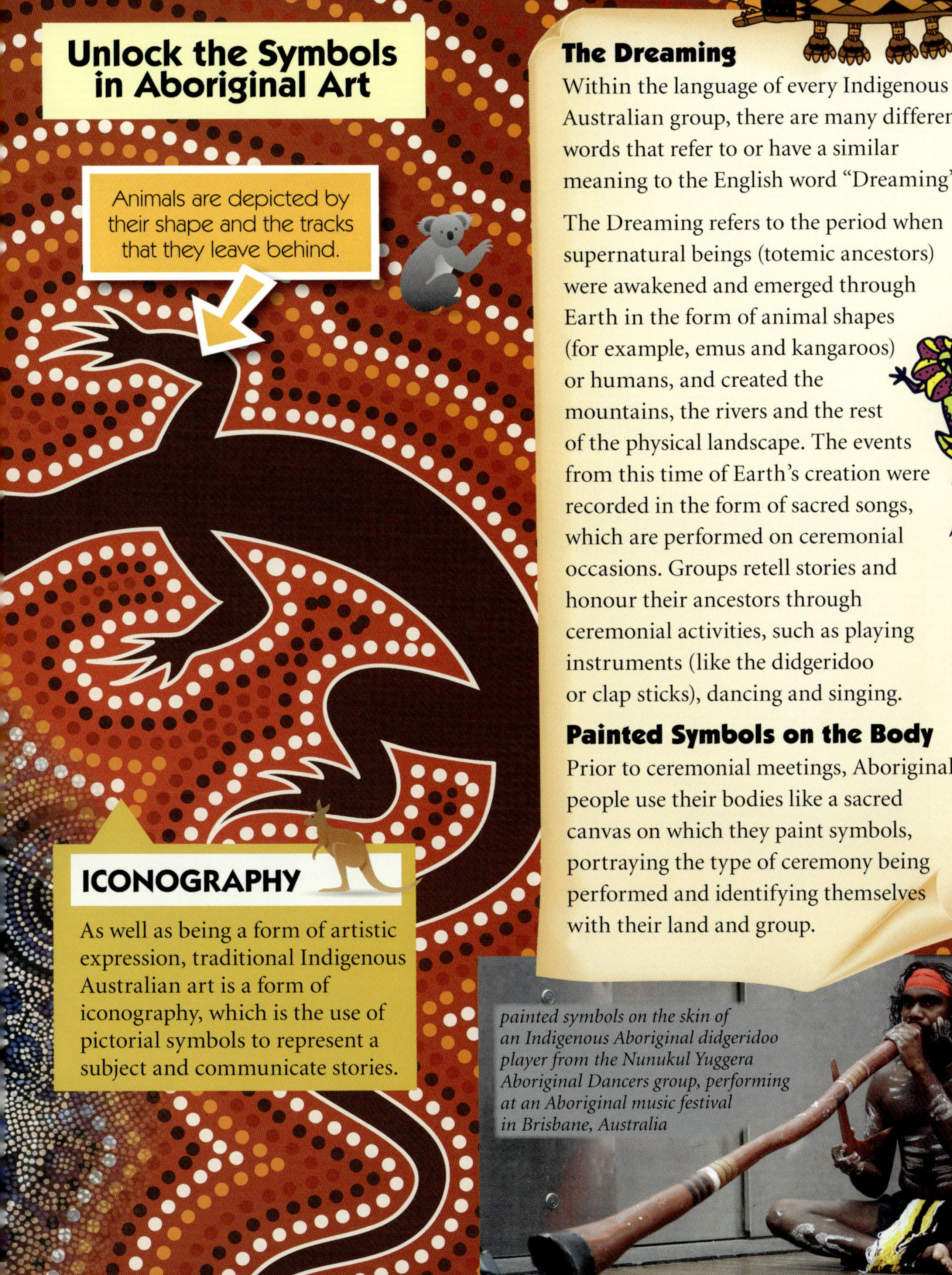

Unlock the Symbols in Aboriginal Art

Animals are depicted by their shape and the tracks that they leave behind.

ICONOGRAPHY

As well as being a form of artistic expression, traditional Indigenous Australian art is a form of iconography, which is the use of pictorial symbols to represent a subject and communicate stories.

The Dreaming

Within the language of every Indigenous Australian group, there are many different words that refer to or have a similar meaning to the English word "Dreaming".

The Dreaming refers to the period when supernatural beings (totemic ancestors) were awakened and emerged through Earth in the form of animal shapes (for example, emus and kangaroos) or humans, and created the mountains, the rivers and the rest of the physical landscape. The events from this time of Earth's creation were recorded in the form of sacred songs, which are performed on ceremonial occasions. Groups retell stories and honour their ancestors through ceremonial activities, such as playing instruments (like the didgeridoo or clap sticks), dancing and singing.

Painted Symbols on the Body

Prior to ceremonial meetings, Aboriginal people use their bodies like a sacred canvas on which they paint symbols, portraying the type of ceremony being performed and identifying themselves with their land and group.

painted symbols on the skin of an Indigenous Aboriginal didgeridoo player from the Nunukul Yuggera Aboriginal Dancers group, performing at an Aboriginal music festival in Brisbane, Australia

Mary Brumby

Mary Brumby (1958–) is an Indigenous Australian artist who lives at Echo Hill, Pukatja Homeland, in northern South Australia. Mary is married with two children and twelve grandchildren. She is Anangu Pitjantjatjara and belongs to the Indulkana and the Mimili communities. Mary enjoys painting, but her artistic talents extend beyond painting to include *tjanpi* (grass weaving), prints, and making jewellery and *punu* (wooden artefacts).

Mary's paintings and other works are displayed at her community's art gallery, Iwantja Arts and Crafts. On most days, Mary works as part of an artistic team at the arts and crafts community centre.

Karu

Karu is an Aboriginal word for "creek". In the painting opposite, a creek bed is the central landscape element. The circular shapes and lines represent the hills and sand hills around the creek. Like all Anangu Pitjantjatjara, Mary has spiritual connections to the ancestral sites in her area and her paintings are a form of expression and historical record.

Whiskey Tjukangku, Anangu Group, works at Iwantja Arts and Crafts

Mary Brumby (right) used traditional symbols and colours to paint Karu, *which symbolises land sacred to her peoples at the Pukatja Homeland. She worked on this painting for one week.*

***Karu* by Mary Brumby**

3 Ancient Art Symbols

The **Petroglyphs** of Edakkal

The Edakkal caves are in the Ambukuthy mountain range in Kerala, India. They are famous for the prehistoric symbols and images that are carved into the rock walls. These rock carvings are called petroglyphs. The earliest petroglyphs at Edakkal are believed to be more than 5 000 years old.

The caves at Edakkal are not true caves, but rather a deep cleft in the rock. A massive boulder fell into the cleft thousands of years ago, and other debris has since built up around it, creating two caves on separate levels. The lower cave is about five-and-a-half metres long and three-and-a-half metres wide, with a roof three metres high. There is a passage opposite the entrance to the lower cave that leads up to a hole in the roof, through which visitors can climb up into the next, higher cave. This one is much larger: 29 metres long and nearly seven metres wide, with a roof five-and-a-half metres high, which is approximately three times the height of a tall person.

carved petroglyphs inside the Edakkal caves

PETROGLYPHS

Petroglyphs are drawings and shapes that have been either drawn or carved onto rock during prehistoric times.

A Symbolic Name

The name Edakkal means “a stone in between”. This describes the way the caves were formed by a large stone that probably detached from the cleft wall, tumbling down until it was trapped between the walls of the fissure.

Legend Carved in Petroglyphs

Local legend tells that it was the mythic figures Lava and Kusha, sons of the great hero Rama, who created the caves by firing arrows into the rock. There is also a legend that Rama himself killed a powerful enemy, Surpanakha, at Edakkal. The stories told by those who created the petroglyphs are not known, however. Their culture and legends can only be guessed at from the carvings they left behind.

Deciphering the Petroglyphs

Inside the caves, the walls are densely and intricately carved. There are so many shapes and lines and figures that they seem to merge together, even though the incisions are still sharp and deep after thousands of years. The most recognisable images in the carvings are human figures. Many of these have striking, raised hair. Some are shown wearing masks. One has a strange blocky head and a spiral body. Another has one very long arm that reaches the ground. One figure of a woman is shown standing on a platform. One male figure would have looked imposingly down on everyone who entered the cave, though now the accumulation of soil over millennia has buried his legs to the knees. All of these details would have been significant to the prehistoric people who carved them, and would have symbolised different things.

There are also many animals carved in the walls. Some resemble animals such as foxes, deer and dogs. One is unmistakably an elephant. These would all have been animals that were significant to the culture of the ancient people of the region. They might have represented particular stories, or they might have symbolised particular qualities. In some cultures foxes represent cleverness or trickery; the foxes carved in the Edakkal caves might have represented these or other characteristics.

Many abstract symbols are carved into the rock, too. These include spirals, stars, wheels, crosses, tridents, common geometric shapes such as triangles, squares and rectangles (some carefully segmented into smaller squares), and a multitude of wavy lines and confusing cross-hatching. Historians and archaeologists are still working to decipher the significance of these. They were clearly symbols intended to convey important practical information and cultural meaning. Those who created and lived among the petroglyphs would likely have been able to interpret these symbols easily on sight.

Culture Preserved in Carvings

The petroglyphs of Edakkal are an extraordinary and beautiful record of the symbols of a prehistoric culture. With careful study, historians and archaeologists can use them to uncover tantalising glimpses into the lives of those who lived at Edakkal thousands of years ago, and carved their history and culture into the walls. But the meaning of the symbols and images will never be fully understood. They are mysteries lost in time, like the people themselves.

4 Cultural Symbols Mark Events

We might say "good luck" to wish someone success or good fortune, but delve into cultures around the world and you will find many symbols believed by people to bring them good luck, too.

Chinese New Year celebrations in Denver, Colorado, USA

Symbol of Red in China

In Chinese culture, the colour red symbolises good fortune and happiness. During times of celebration, such as Chinese New Year, red is the dominant colour used to wish people good fortune and health in the future and as an expression of joy. A long-practised Chinese tradition is for families to exchange red envelopes containing a little money. Usually, married adults and the elderly give red envelopes to children to protect them from evil and symbolise a new year of good health.

WHITE NOT RED

In Chinese culture, white, not red or black, is the respectful colour at funerals.

A Chinese dragon enthralls crowds in Argentina celebrating Chinese New Year.

a family at Chinese New Year with their lucky red envelopes

Chinese Zodiac

The Chinese Zodiac (*Sheng Xiao* in Chinese) uses twelve animal signs to mark the rotating twelve-year cycle of the Chinese calendar. The Chinese year is based on the cycles of the moon, and therefore Chinese New Year (Lunar New Year) can begin anywhere between late January and the middle of February in the Western calendar (also called the Gregorian calendar). It is traditionally believed in Chinese culture that people born in the year of a particular animal have certain character traits, behaviours and fortune (good or bad) that differentiate them from people born in other years.

GREGORIAN CALENDAR

In China, people use the internationally recognised Gregorian calendar (1 January to 31 December) for business and communication within the global community.

AN EXAMPLE 2000–2013

Signs of the **Western Zodiac**

In Western astrology and astronomy, the zodiac refers to the band of space through which the Sun appears to move over the course of a year. The path the Sun takes passes through a different one of 12 constellations every month. These constellations are the signs of the zodiac. The signs of the zodiac each have a human figure or animal associated with them. The zodiac starts with Aries (ram), and continues in order with Taurus (bull), Gemini (twins), Cancer (crab), Leo (lion), Virgo (virgin), Libra (balance, symbolised by a set of scales), Scorpio (scorpion), Sagittarius (archer, represented by a centaur with a bow), Capricorn (goat or sea-goat), Aquarius (water bearer) and Pisces (fish). As with the Chinese zodiac, Western astrology holds that people born under certain zodiac signs have particular personality traits and behaviours. For example, Libra, representing balance, means that people born under this sign are believed to be better able to express balanced points of view.

ZODIAC IN GREEK

In Greek language, the translation for zodiac is "circle of animals".

Symbols of Birthstones

Birthstones are gemstones associated with the months of the year. There has been a long tradition of people wearing jewellery made with birthstones in the belief they will bring good fortune, protection and health.

Over the centuries, many gemstones have been used as birthstones for each month. Here are some popular gems symbolising birthdays today:

January:	Garnet	July:	Ruby
February:	Amethyst	August:	Peridot
March:	Aquamarine	September:	Sapphire
April:	Diamond	October:	Opal
May:	Emerald	November:	Topaz
June:	Moonstone	December:	Turquoise

ANNIVERSARIES

Certain gemstones mark milestone anniversaries, e.g. the ruby is a symbol for a 40th wedding anniversary, and the sapphire symbolises a 45th wedding anniversary.

A Key Birthday

21st Birthday:
A key can be a symbol of having reached adulthood, and is often given to people turning 21. This represents their right to come and go from the family home as they like.

Matrimonial Symbols

Engagement Ring: Worn by women on their left ring finger, an engagement ring is a symbol of an intention to marry soon.

Wedding Ring: Traditionally a symbol of marriage, wedding rings are worn by both wife and husband on the left ring finger.

A Clannagh Ring: In Ireland, clannagh rings worn with the heart inwards is a symbol that the wearer is in a relationship or married.

Bindi:
In India, married women apply a red colour, or bindi, on the forehead or along the parting of the hair as a symbol of their marital status.

5 Is a Logo a Symbol?

The design of a logo may include a symbol. Over time, the public may see a symbol used so often in various marketing activities that they recognise the logo as the "name" of a company or organisation.

As a graphically designed element, a logo is a powerful tool for representing a product, a place or an organisation. A logo consists of the full or abbreviated name of a company, or a symbol, or both.

TRADEMARK

A trademark, or brand, is a symbol that identifies a product or service of a particular company, to distinguish it from other companies. Trademarks are usually registered with official government authorities in one or more countries.

Some Common Logo Symbols

the "copyright" symbol, which means a logo cannot be copied without permission from the owner

the "registered" symbol, which means a logo is registered with a government authority

TM *the "trademarked" symbol, which means a logo cannot be used by any other company or individual*

Logos for Marketing

Logos are used for all kinds of marketing materials, from small business cards and email address signatures to large flags and billboards. A logo should leave people with a favourable impression of the company and their product or service.

Business Cards

Letterheads

Envelopes

Billboard

Designing Effective Logos

An effective logo must represent the product, service or company it is associated with simply and clearly, so that people can easily recognise and remember it. It is important to create simplicity with bold lines and one or two strong-looking elements so that the logo can be reproduced clearly whether in colour or in black and white, and at any size.

Stage 1
Brainstorm and sketch out your ideas.

Stage 2
Develop your ideas, experimenting with colour and detail.

Stage 3
Develop your best idea with variations of font and layout and choose your favourite version.

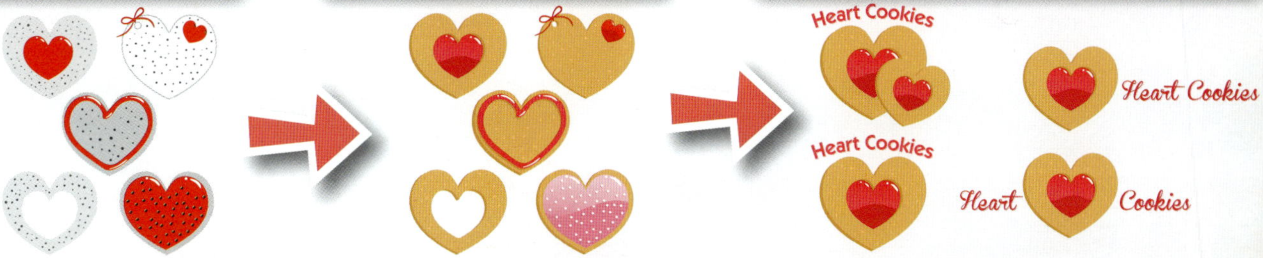

Heart Cookies
Heart Cookies
Heart Cookies
Heart
Cookies

Balance
When you are creating and designing a logo, make sure that it looks balanced.

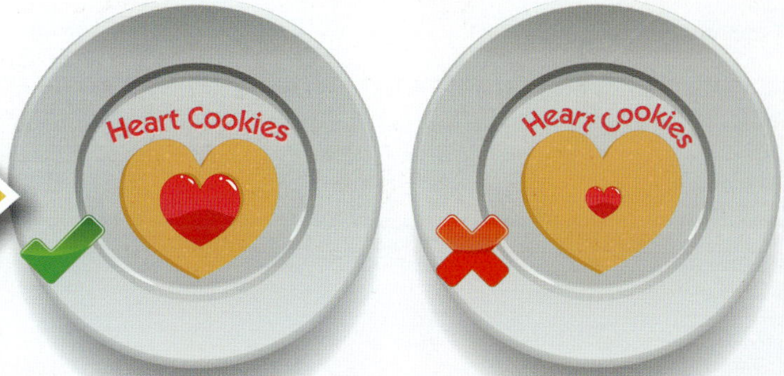

Heart Cookies
Heart Cookies

I U
This Valentine's Day say it with love.
Say it with Heart Cookies.
Love
Special-Edition Cookies

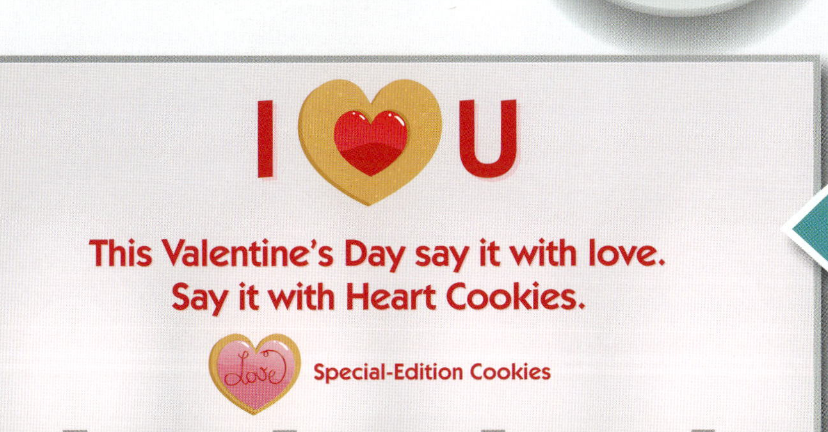

Visual Impact for a Large Billboard
Use consistent style, fonts, colours and a clear logo.

6 Symbols from the Heart

The heart is one of the most popular symbols. It is used in all kinds of ways and places. People in many different cultures instantly recognise and comprehend the meaning of the heart symbol.

Red Heart Symbol

A red heart has a universal meaning of love and affection. It is particularly associated with Valentine's Day.

Blue Heart Symbol

A blue heart could be used to show that people care about the world's oceans.

A Heart of Gold Symbol

When someone says, "You have a heart of gold", it means that you are very kind, thoughtful and helpful.

Pink Heart Symbol

The idiom "in the pink" means that you are in good health, so a pink heart could be used to symbolise a health project or product.

Green Heart Symbol

When the colour of a heart symbol is changed to green, it takes on a slightly different meaning. A green heart is often used to convey a love for the environment or for an environmentally friendly practice such as recycling.

brochure designed by Green Hearts Recyclers

logo for Green Hearts Recyclers

Wearing red plastic noses is a symbol of support on Red Nose Day for SIDS and Kids.

Green Hearts Recyclers

Green Hearts Recyclers is a not-for-profit organisation in Australia that recycles waste products from companies and redirects the funds to support five different charities. One of the charities is SIDS and Kids, based in Victoria, Australia. The symbol for this charity is a red nose, which people wear or display on Red Nose Day (the last Friday in June).

Social Studies

SIDS and Kids

SIDS stands for "Sudden Infant Death Syndrome". SIDS and Kids was first formed in 1978 to fund research into why babies can die suddenly and unexpectedly and to provide community education that helps prevent these deaths.

7 Signing Symbols

Sign language enables communication among people who are deaf, have significant hearing loss or have speech disabilities. Signing provides a common language for effective communication between people with and without hearing or speech disabilities. In Australia, Auslan (Australian Sign Language) is the most commonly used signing language.

Eat more, drink, sleep? I don't need an interpreter to obey those commands!

Communication

National Interpreter Symbol

In Australia, the National Interpreter Symbol was created in 2006. It clearly indicates to people of non-English-speaking backgrounds where to find interpreter services in public places, such as hospitals.

Auslan Alphabet Chart

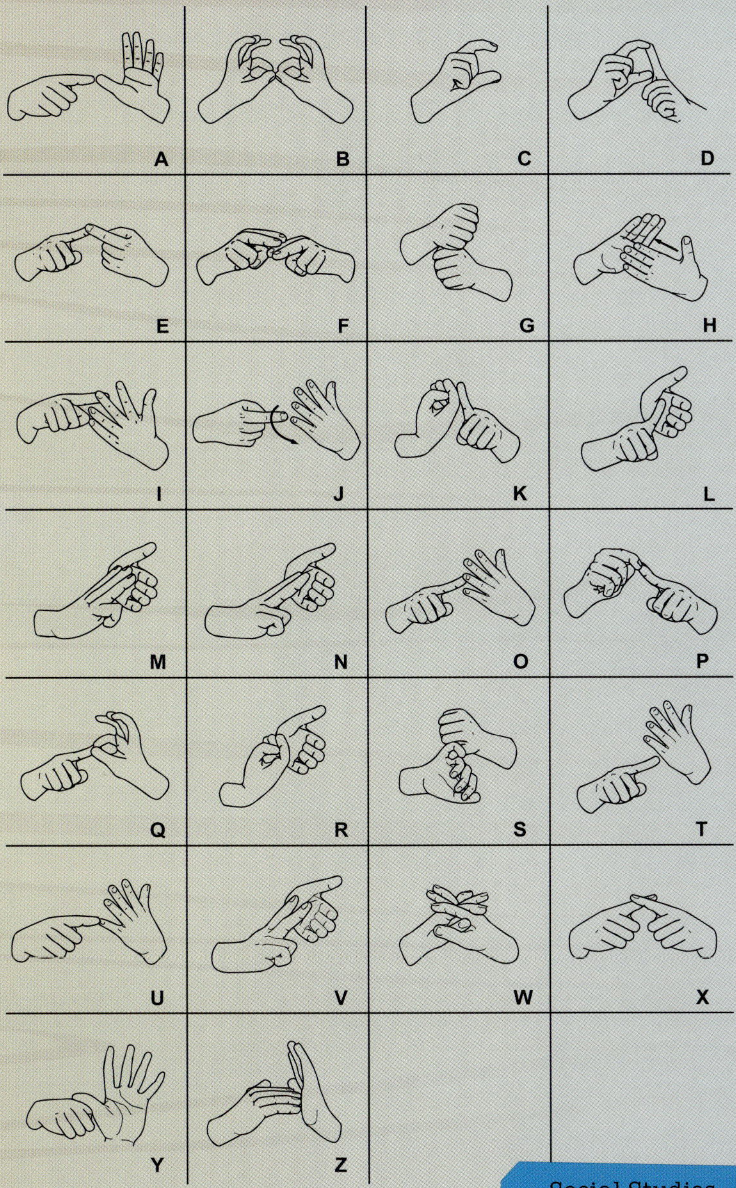

A	B	C	D
E	F	G	H
I	J	K	L
M	N	O	P
Q	R	S	T
U	V	W	X
Y	Z		

Social Studies

A Speech Pathologist

Formerly known as a speech therapist, a speech pathologist has an extensive range of skills to assess and treat people with all kinds of communication difficulties (e.g. speech, writing and reading), physical functions (e.g. swallowing food) and comprehending non-verbal communication (e.g. symbols, signs, gestures).

Symbol of Care

A common symbol used in medicine is a stylised Rod of Asclepius. This is a rod encircled with a snake, which the Ancient Greeks believed was used by Asclepius, a god associated with healing and medicine. Often, doctors, hospitals and pharmacies will display this symbol.

8 Writing Symbols

Letters and words are symbols that have long formed the basis of written communication. But go back in time and you will discover cultures in which people communicated stories and information through symbols and figures, as well as through oral narratives passed down from generation to generation. In recent times, linguists have worked with many indigenous groups to help create a written language that will enable their oral language and culture to be recorded and preserved for future generations.

Written **Communication** Timeline

4000 BCE – clay tablet

1300 BCE – stylus

600 AD – quill

1790s – pencil

1830s – nib pen

1880s – fountain pen

1940s – ballpoint pen

1990s – laptop computer

Today – smart phone

Writing Symbols for Greeting Friends

Japanese Writing **Symbols**

Japanese writing characters are beautifully crafted artistic symbols. There are three systems of writing Japanese in modern Japan, each with its own alphabet. The Japanese alphabet of *katakana* is used mainly for foreign words, and *kana* comprises two main forms of writing.

Kana

The writing system called *kana* consists of symbols that represent the sounds of words. There are two main forms of *kana* used in Japan: *kanji* and *hiragana*. In *kanji* and *hiragana*, the word sounds the same, but the way it is represented by symbols is different.

Communication

Oldest Writing System

Chinese characters form the oldest continuous system of written communication in the world. There are thousands of characters.

Chinese symbol for peace

Kanji
In *kanji* a single symbol is used to represent the whole word and all its syllables. *Kanji* originally developed from Chinese symbols called *hanzi*.

Hiragana
In *hiragana*, a group of symbols, one for each syllable in the word, is used.

Compare Japanese Writing Symbols for Parts of the Body

Kanji	Hiragana	Pronunciation	English
首	くび	***kubi***	**neck**
唇	くちびる	***kuchibiru***	**lips**
鼻	はな	***hana***	**nose**
目	め	***me***	**eye**
耳	みみ	***mimi***	**ear**
額	ひたい	***hitai***	**forehead**

9 Symbols of Countries

Governments use symbols that are meaningful to their people when they commission designers to create official items, such as flags and emblems. The symbols are drawn from the country's indigenous cultures, natural and human-made landmarks, native animals and plants, and landscapes.

Symbols of Australia

Some of the more internationally recognisable symbols of Australia are described here.

Native Animals: Koala and Kangaroo

Landscape Landmark: Uluru

Natural Stone: Opal

OPAL IN ABORIGINAL DREAMING STORY

The Wangkumara people in western New South Wales, Australia, have a Dreaming story that tells how a pelican helped them obtain fire from opals.

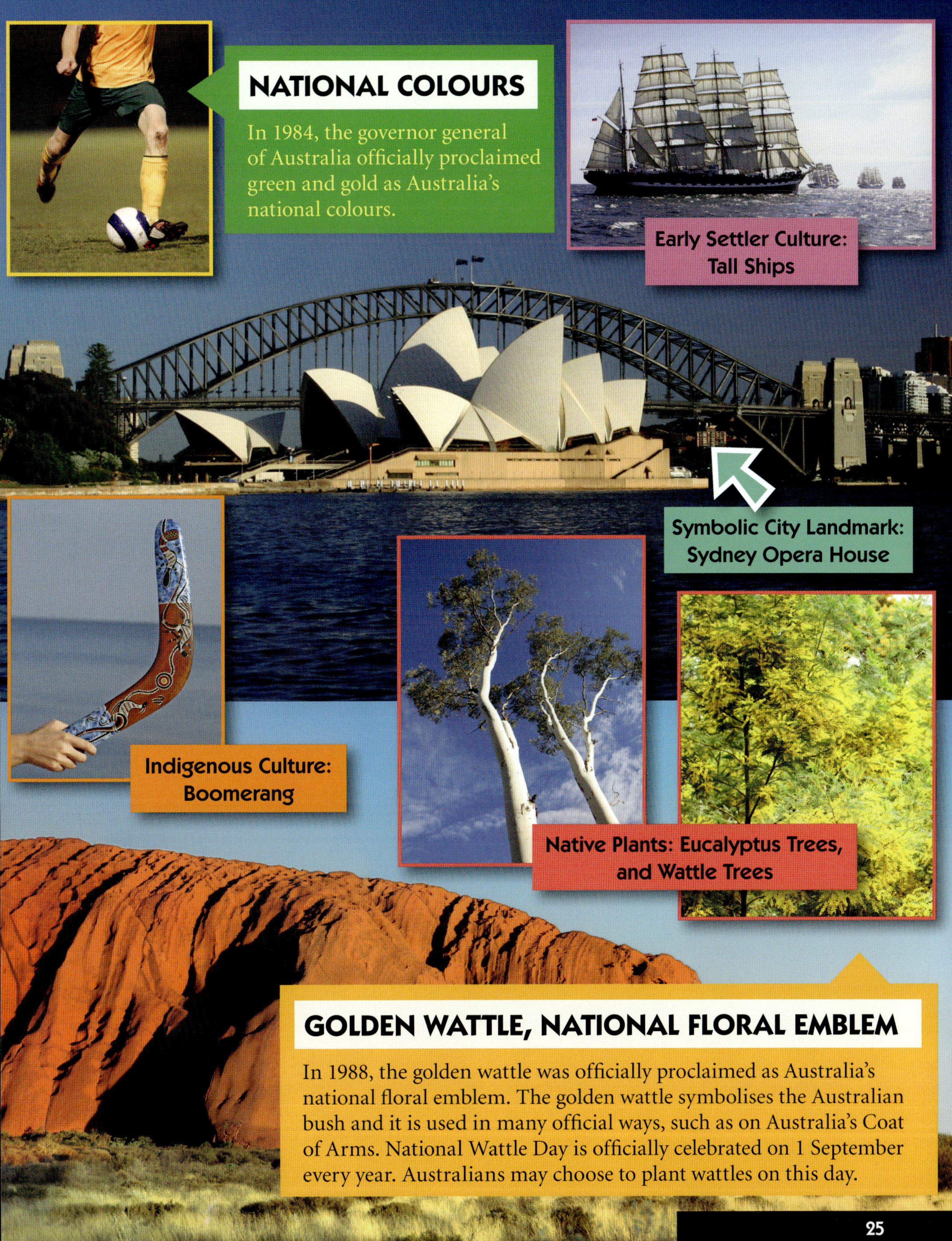

NATIONAL COLOURS

In 1984, the governor general of Australia officially proclaimed green and gold as Australia's national colours.

Early Settler Culture: Tall Ships

Symbolic City Landmark: Sydney Opera House

Indigenous Culture: Boomerang

Native Plants: Eucalyptus Trees, and Wattle Trees

GOLDEN WATTLE, NATIONAL FLORAL EMBLEM

In 1988, the golden wattle was officially proclaimed as Australia's national floral emblem. The golden wattle symbolises the Australian bush and it is used in many official ways, such as on Australia's Coat of Arms. National Wattle Day is officially celebrated on 1 September every year. Australians may choose to plant wattles on this day.

Animals Become National Symbols

The top ten foreign countries in which Australians were born, according to Australia's 2011 Census, are shown on the map. Check out the chart listing the countries in order of population size along with their national animals, which have been used in various symbolic forms. These are just some of the symbolic ways the animals are portrayed.

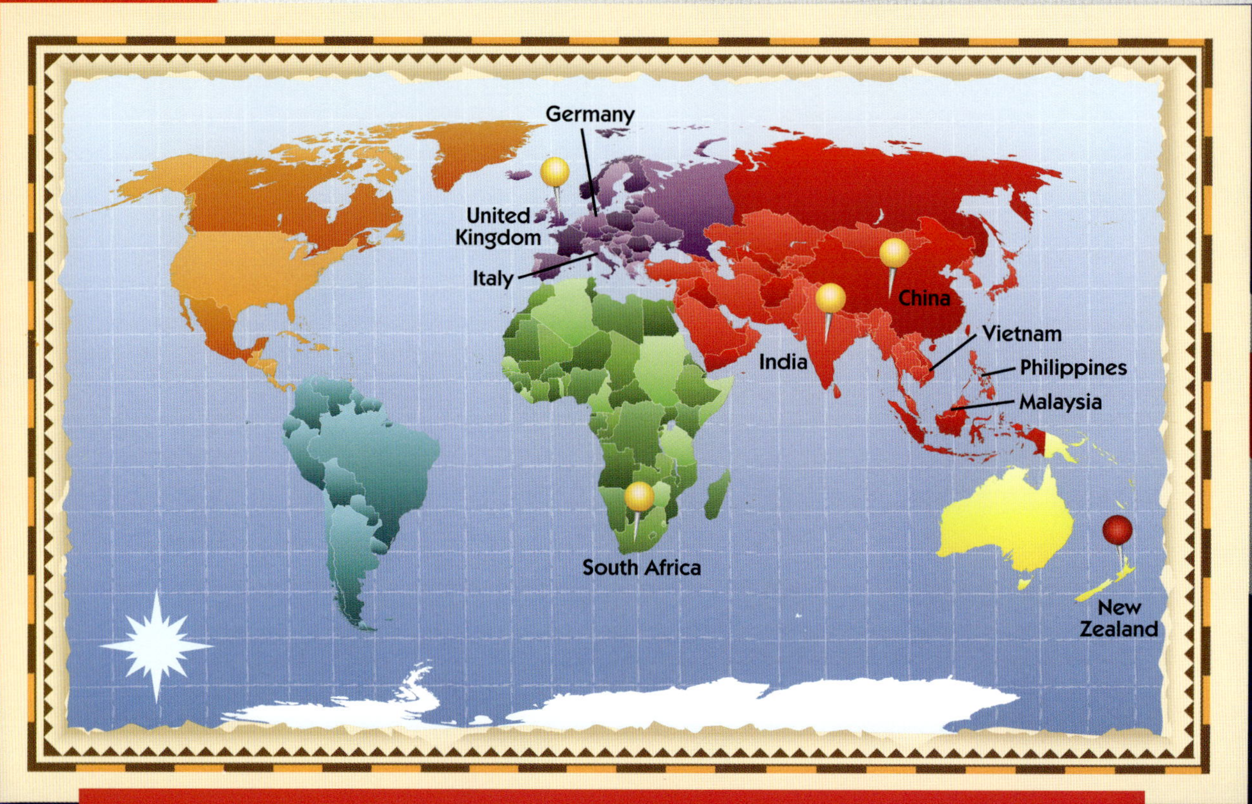
Germany
United Kingdom
Italy
China
India
Vietnam
Philippines
Malaysia
South Africa
New Zealand

Top 10 Nationalities in Australia and their Animal Symbols

1

DIEU
ET MON
DROIT

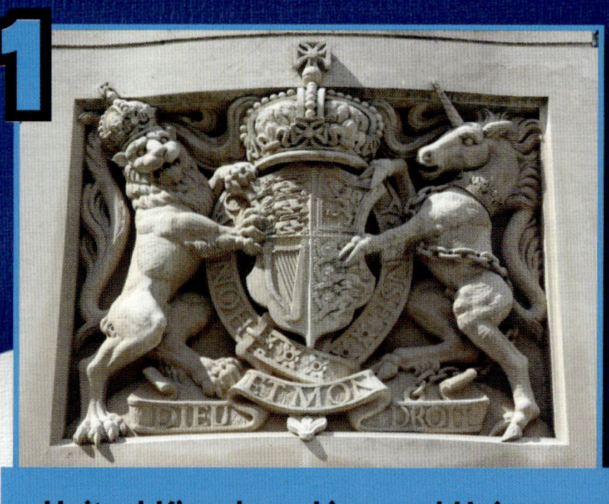

United Kingdom: Lion and Unicorn

2

ONE DOLLAR

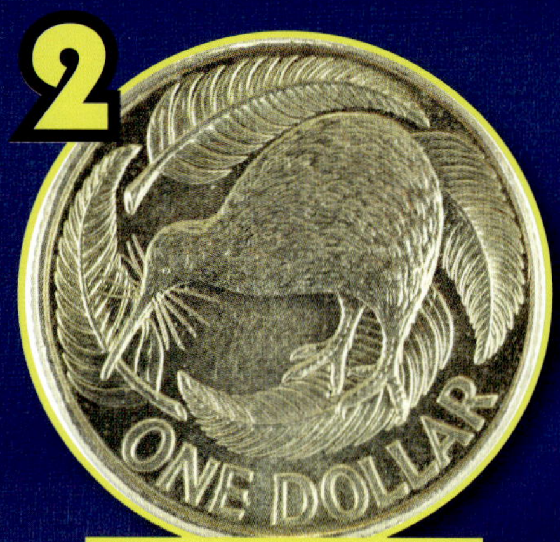

New Zealand: Kiwi

3

China: Giant Panda

an example of an advertisment featuring a panda

4

India: Royal Bengal Tiger

5

Italy: Italian Wolf

6

Vietnam: Water Buffalo (and the tiger and dragon)

7

Philippines: Carabao

8

South Africa: Springbok

9

Malaysia: Malayan Tiger

10

Germany: Black Eagle

an example of an advertisment with a tiger theme

10 Geographical and Landmark Symbols

GIBNA DOMIATI

Gibna Domiati is a white soft cheese made in the north of Egypt. It is usually made from buffalo milk but occasionally cow's milk is added to the mixture, too. It is Egypt's most common cheese and is used in a lot of recipes.

PANINI

The English translation of the Italian word *panini* is sandwiches. A single sandwich is a *panino*.

Pop Into Italy for...

Pizza

Panini

Pasta

PARIS, A PERFECT PLACE FOR A PLATE OF PETITS FOURS!

PETITS FOURS

The English translation of the French term *petits fours* is "small ovens". *Petits fours* are small, square-cut cakes or confectionary, usually served after a main course as a dessert.

Colosseum, Italy
Statue of Liberty, the USA
Stonehenge, England
Acropolis, Greece
Taj Mahal, India
The Great Wall of China, China

11 Designing Currency Symbols

India's Currency Symbol

In July 2010, the Finance Ministry of the Indian Government announced the winner of a competition to design the symbol for their national currency, the rupee. The purpose of the competition was to design a meaningful and distinctive-looking currency symbol that would visually distinguish it from rupee currency codes and symbols used by other Asian countries. India's new currency symbol:

- clearly distinguishes India's rupee from the rupee currency symbols of other countries
- resembles other major currency symbols around the world
- makes it easier for people to identify it as a symbol of currency than the international standard three-letter currency code "INR" did.

India's new rupee banknotes feature Mahatma Gandhi (1869–1948). Gandhi was a highly respected leader who campaigned peacefully and diplomatically for the freedom, civil rights and independence of Indian people.

The vertical line of a capital "R" was removed

The symbol resembles "Ra" in the Indian alphabet Devanagari

The horizontal line aligning with the top line creates a similar "look" to other currency symbols such as the euro, the British pound and the Japanese yen.

Europe's Currency Symbol

On 1 January 2002, the first euro notes and coins entered circulation in 12 member states of the EU. A design competition was held to find the best design for the euro's currency symbol. The European Commission made the ultimate decision.

The euro is the official currency of the countries belonging to the European Union (EU), which include Germany, France, Italy, Netherlands and Spain. Currently 10 EU countries are not using the euro. An exception is the United Kingdom, which joined the EU but continued to use its British currency.

Euro Symbol

The curved "E" represents the first letter in "Europe" and was inspired by the Greek Epsilon, which is the fifth letter of the Greek alphabet.

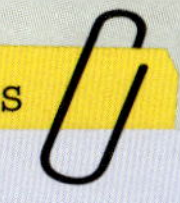

Social Studies

European Commission

The European Commission represents the EU as a whole. It is governed by a group of 27 commissioners – one representative from each of the member countries. The European Commission works to ensure that the laws of the EU are properly followed by all of the EU countries.

The **Greenback** $US

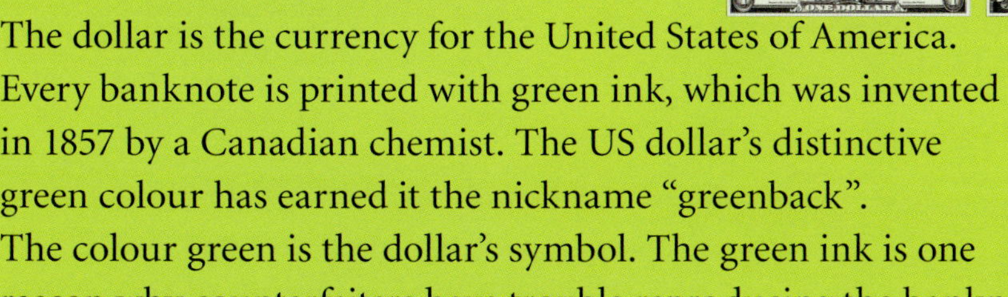

The dollar is the currency for the United States of America. Every banknote is printed with green ink, which was invented in 1857 by a Canadian chemist. The US dollar's distinctive green colour has earned it the nickname "greenback". The colour green is the dollar's symbol. The green ink is one reason why counterfeiters have trouble reproducing the banknotes.

banknotes for the USA and India

$ Symbol in Other Countries

Many other countries have adopted a dollar as the unit of their own currency. Australia, New Zealand, Canada, Hong Kong and many Pacific countries use dollars. Although they are all different to the US dollar, the symbol is the same. Banks and other financial institutions use a country code after the dollar symbol to ensure that different currencies with the same name are not confused.

$AUS

$CAN

$NZD

$HKD

In most countries now, the dollar symbol has only one bar through the S-shape, but in the USA it is common to use two bars. The dollar sign is a universal symbol that almost everyone recognises.

Index

Glossary

accumulation A collecting together of something over time

Auslan Australian Sign Language, used by people with hearing difficulties

commission To pay someone to perform a service, e.g. to create an artwork

counterfeiters People who create imitations that are intended to pass as originals, usually for financial gain

decipher To make out the meaning of something

interpret To translate something from one means of communication to another, e.g. from one language to another, or from music to words

linguists Specialists in the study of languages

petroglyphs Drawings or carvings on rock

stylised To make something conform to a conventional style or appearance, so it is simplified and easily recognisable

totemic Representative or emblematic of a family, tribe or related group